Date Due

SEP 2 8 1976		
NOV 1 7 1976		
JAN 1 8 1980		
JUN 1 3 1980		
JUN 1 8 1982		
AUG 2 4 1989 1989		
SEP 0 7 1989		
MAR 0 8 1990		

The
Queen Who Couldn't
Bake Gingerbread

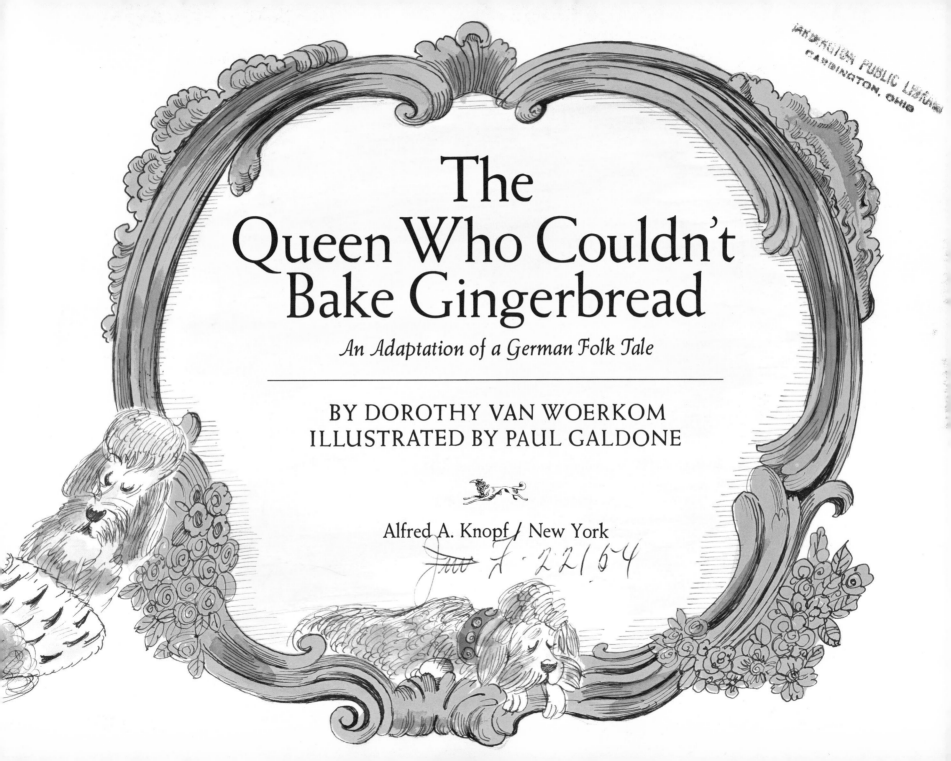

The Queen Who Couldn't Bake Gingerbread

An Adaptation of a German Folk Tale

BY DOROTHY VAN WOERKOM
ILLUSTRATED BY PAUL GALDONE

Alfred A. Knopf / New York

For Donna and Ed

This is a Borzoi Book published by Alfred A. Knopf, Inc. Text Copyright © 1975 by Dorothy Van Woerkom. Illustrations Copyright © 1975 by Paul Galdone. All rights reserved under International and Pan-American Copyright Conventions. Published in the United States by Alfred A. Knopf, Inc., New York, and simultaneously in Canada by Random House of Canada Limited, Toronto. Distributed by Random House, Inc., New York. Manufactured in the United States of America. *Library of Congress Cataloging in Publication Data* Van Woerkom, Dorothy. The queen who couldn't bake gingerbread. SUMMARY: When the King of Mulligatawny is unable to find a queen who bakes gingerbread, he finally realizes there are more important things to consider in selecting a wife. [1. Folklore—Germany. 2. Fairy tales.] I. Galdone, Paul, illus. II. Title. PZ8.1.V457Qe 398.2'2'0943 [E] 74-15302 ISBN 0-394-83033-4 ISBN 0-394-93033-9 (lib. bdg.) 0 9 8 7 6 5 4 3 2 1

King Pilaf

of Mulligatawny was having a very bad day.
To begin with, he bumped his head against the
Lord Chamberlain's upon getting out of bed.
Then he discovered a hole in the heel of his
stocking that was the size of a marble.

And he knew without asking that his breakfast gingerbread would be crumbly again.

The King sat on the edge of his bed with his thumb through the hole in his stocking.

"It is time," he said to the Lord Chamberlain, "that Mulligatawny had a Queen and I a wife. She must be beautiful enough to please me. She must be wise enough to help me rule—and to find me a tailor who knows how to MEND."

The Lord Chamberlain slipped the King's stocking over the Royal foot.

"A splendid idea, your Majesty!" he said. "By happy chance I was thinking the very same thing myself. As a matter of fact..."

The King wagged his foot under the Lord Chamberlain's nose and sighed loudly. "Not one of your speeches so early in the day, my Lord. Just help me into my boots, and let's have some breakfast."

So they drank their lime juice and ate cheese omelet, with ginger-bread that crumbled. The King frowned at the crumbs on his plate and said, "My Queen must be *more* than just wise and beautiful. She must also know how to bake gingerbread."

Now it was the Lord Chamberlain who sighed. For when Pilaf became King, he had turned Mulligatawny inside out to find a gingerbread baker.

"There isn't one in my kingdom who can bake it to a turn," the King was saying. "It should be neither too hard nor too soft, but just properly crisp."

Then he called for their horses, and away they rode to the kingdom of Ghur, where there lived a Princess as wise as she was beautiful. Her name was Madelon.

"No, I cannot bake gingerbread," Princess Madelon said. "But I make perfect little almond cakes."

King Pilaf thought about that: a Queen both wise and beautiful, who could make pretty cakes. But at last he shook his head sadly, and kissed Princess Madelon's hand.

"I'm sorry to say that it must be gingerbread," he said.

Then off he galloped with the Lord Chamberlain to the kingdom of Shoggen.

Here lived a Princess who was not as wise as she was beautiful. Her name was Jebelle.

"No, I cannot bake gingerbread," said Princess Jebelle. "But I can bake the best zwieback that you will ever taste."

Princess Jebelle would make a beautiful Queen. But *zwieback*—no, the King could never like zwieback at all.

"I'm sorry to say that it must be gingerbread," he said.

King Pilaf kissed her hand and rode away with his Chamberlain to the kingdom of Tintinnabulum.

Here lived a Princess who was not as beautiful as she was wise. Her name was Calliope.

"Ah, King Pilaf!" Princess Calliope cried, as the King strode into her chamber. "You are, I suppose, seeking a wife?"

"I am, indeed, your Highness. A wife who can bake gingerbread and who…"

"Oh no, I *never* bake gingerbread. But I am seeking a husband. He must be as kind as he is handsome, and he must know how to play on the slide trombone."

For a moment the King's mouth made an "O" like the hole in the heel of his stocking.

"I cannot play on the slide trombone," he said
at last. "But I can shoot an arrow as straight
as the tail of a comet." He took a deep breath.

"Then I'm sorry to say," said the Princess,
"that the husband for me is the man who can
play on the slide trombone."

Her smile made him wish he could say, "Yes,
I can!" But all he could do was bow himself out,
and take to his horse once again.

Now, in every single kingdom it was the same: no one at all could bake a proper gingerbread. King Pilaf kissed the hand of the very last Princess. He called for his horse and rode home with his Chamberlain, to brood.

After quite a long while (a hole had now appeared in the heel of his other stocking—and he had never felt so lonely, besides!) he said, "Lord Chamberlain, it is plain to see that I must do without gingerbread. Go back to the kingdom of Ghur and ask the Princess Madelon if she will marry me. She is as wise as she is beautiful, and perhaps in time I can learn to like almond cakes."

When the Lord Chamberlain arrived in Ghur, he found the kingdom prepared for a wedding.

The Princess was going to marry the King of Rocky Knob Island!

"Well," said King Pilaf, when he heard about this, "you must go to the kingdom of Shoggen. Princess Jebelle is not as wise as she is beautiful, but perhaps in time I can learn to like zwieback."

The Lord Chamberlain soon returned with news that Princess
Jebelle had left a note on her crown for her father. She had run off with
a sourdough baker and was baking miles of zwieback.

King Pilaf surprised the Lord Chamberlain by dancing a jig when he heard about Princess Jebelle.

"To tell you the truth, my Lord," he said, "I like Princess Calliope best. She is not as beautiful, of course, as she is wise. But then, what chance have I, since I cannot play on the slide trombone?"

"As a matter of fact," the Lord Chamberlain said, "I was thinking of Princess Calliope, too. She is, as you say, very wise. Perhaps she knows what can be done."

"Excellent advice!" cried the King. "I shall go to see her at once."

When Princess Calliope heard why King
Pilaf had come, she said, "Let me think about
this. I am sure we can come to some sort of
agreement."

He paced up and down outside of her chamber, until at last she came to the door.

"It seems to me," she said with a bow, "that
a husband who is as kind as he is handsome
is more to be loved than one who can play on
the slide trombone."

"And a wife who is wise," the King said quickly, "as well as—er beautiful, does not need to know how to bake gingerbread."

They clasped hands together, and Calliope said, "Then let us add this to our marriage vows: we must never again mention *slide trombone*..."

"Or *gingerbread*!" he finished, with a laugh that shook the walls of the castle.

They lived happily together for nearly a year, and ruled their kingdom as well as anyone could.

Until one day, when everything went wrong. The King dropped the crown on his foot, and the Queen awoke with a headache. The Lord Chamberlain was ill, and the cook slept late. The court painter put his head through their Majesties' new portrait, and the Queen's dog chewed up all the paintbrushes. Outside, it snowed one minute and rained the next.

The King was angry; the Queen was cross. They quarrelled all day.

"I wish," the King shouted, "that you could bake gingerbread! Then SOMETHING would be right about this terrible day."

"And why," cried the Queen, "can't YOU play on the slide trombone? It would certainly help to calm my nerves!"

They glared at each other with anger and spite. The forbidden words had been said, their marriage vow broken.

They both turned around and swept from the room, to the opposite ends of their castle.

They stayed there for days, feeling grumpy and sorry for themselves. Servants left food on trays near their doors, then scampered away before the door might open.

The citizens of Mulligatawny began to ask each other, "What has gone wrong at the Castle?"

At last, Queen Calliope looked at herself in her mirror. "The King married me because I was wise, not beautiful," she said. "Now, was it wise to shout SLIDE TROMBONE at him?"

It was not. She sent for the Lord Chamberlain.

At the other end of the castle, King Pilaf was trying to shave himself.
"With that nose and those eyes," he said to the King in the mirror,
"you are not nearly so handsome as you like to believe."

He wiped blood from the cut on his chin. "Why, the Queen married
me because she thought I was kind! Was it kind to shout
GINGERBREAD?"

He struck off the last whisker and sent for the Lord Chamberlain.

Before very long, from one end of the castle came the odor of scorched pots. From the other came sounds like an elephant blowing its nose.

The servants rushed in one direction holding their ears; in the other they rushed holding their breath.

The citizens of Mulligatawny thought the world was coming to an end.

But then, in the middle of one night, the smells grew sweeter. At the very same time, the sounds became more tuneful. The servants hurried about with noses high in the air to smell the delicious smells. They paused in their work to hear the sweet sounds.

The citizens of Mulligatawny began to hope for the future.

At last, the Lord Chamberlain announced that their Majesties would come from their opposite sides of the castle and meet in the Great Hall.

With a blast of trumpets, the door at one end of the Great Hall swung open. In marched the King, with an apron around his middle, a baker's hat on his head, and flour on his nose. He carried a pan of the most perfect gingerbread that had ever been baked in his kingdom—or in any other.

Without any sound at all, the doors at the other end of the Great Hall opened. Through them stepped the Queen. She raised a slide trombone to her lips, and played such a melody that even the nightingales hushed.

From that very day, the first sound heard each morning in
Mulligatawny was Queen Calliope's slide trombone. The first scent
was that of King Pilaf's fresh gingerbread. It became the custom of the
citizens to awake at sunrise, to sniff and to listen. Their noses and their
ears would tell them if all was still well in the kingdom.

To the end of their days, they were never disappointed.